SOARING SPIRIT

A TEACHER OF TRUST

ANGELA WARREN

SOARING SPIRIT

A Teacher Of Trust

For my wonderful children and inspiration:
Kody, Karly, Allyson, and Alexander.
May we continue to soar together.
Special thanks go to Allyson and Alexander
for your help in making this book amazing
~AW~

Table of Contents

Chapter 1

The Storm

The darkness was not the only thing the night brought on this stormy evening. Heavy rain was falling fast and hard.

It sounded like large buckets of water being poured on the house. Along with the heavy, fast, and hard rain, the wind was gusting so rigid and loud. You could hear the trees bending and cracking.

We sat there wondering if the next sound was going to be a tree-branch falling on the roof. Time seemed to stand still in this unmerciful storm.

There was not much we could do but sleep the night away and hope when we awake we would find everything in tacked.

When we wok the next morning, there was a scary silence that resonated in the air. But we knew that the night's violent storm did not leave without making its presence known.

As I walked outside, I was not expecting the mess I discovered. There were leaves and tree branches, both big and small scattered all around the yard. The trampoline that was securely set in the yard was flipped onto its side.

It would take more than myself to lift our trampoline, so I asked my oldest daughter, Ilya Marie to help me.

Ilya went on one side of the trampoline while I was on the other. As Ilya nearly reached the other side she came running back over me, frightened, saying, *"I am not going over there!"*

I asked her what was wrong, and she simply said, *"Go over there, and you will see."* I was thinking to myself, "The storm left big and small tree branches on the ground to pick up, and flipped over the trampoline.

What else did the night storm leave behind?"

Chapter 2

Beginning of Trust

I walked over to where Ilya was and on the ground in front of me was a beautiful falcon, with his wings out in defense.

The windy storm must have blown so hard that he was thrown to the ground and wounded. I was not sure what to do.

By the way he was acting, I knew he was very distraught and afraid. I could only think of one thing to do.

I got my gloves on, knelled, looked him in the eyes and began speaking softly to him. I told him, *"I will help you, but you must trust me, and I will trust you"*.

All the while, I was thinking, what are you doing? This is a wild and hurt falcon. He does not feel safe and I am sure he does not understand anything I am saying".

To my surprise, he slowly lowered his wings and waddled right up to me. He then perched on my hand ever so gently.

It was like he knew that I only wanted to help him and it seemed he understood my words.

At first, I was standing there not wanting to make any sudden moves. Then I realized, I have a wild beautiful falcon perched on my hand.

Somehow, he seemed to understand what I was saying, and now he was on my hand, expecting me to live up to my words of helping him.

I walked around the house to the front where the closed-in porch is. As we were walking together, we were just looking at each other, we both had a look that said, *"Is this really happening.?"* or perhaps we each were waiting for one sudden wrong move from each other.

As we arrived to the front porch, I lowered my hand to the railing so that he could sit on it. He slowly moved from my hand onto the railing. I could feel that we both were a little relieved.

We followed through on trusting each other. Now we both were relaxed. Well at least for a minute.

Chapter 3

Whats for Dinner

It did not take long for him to feel safe enough to start making demands. Maybe not in the language I would understand, but in bird language with his screeching bird call.

Now I had the task of trying to figure out what he wanted. I tried water, nope not it. I tried placing him on something more comfortable, still not the solution.

Then it came to me: FOOD! That is what he wanted.

Now the next challenge: what does a Falcon eat? Hmmm, peanut butter and jelly? Pizza? Mac and cheese?

No, not any of those. Oh! I know! Meat, he needed meat. So off to the refrigerator I went. Just what the doctor ordered for my new-found friend, chicken meat.

Boy, he must have been hungry. I didn't even get a chance to place it on the ground before he approached me and ate it right our of my hand.

It did not take long for him to finish his meal, and he was ready for a nap.

This was the start of an amazing experience for both the Warren family and the Falcon.

Chapter 4

Family Bonding

T he next morning, I awoke to a squawking sound which came from my porch. I laid there thinking, "what is on my porch"?

I jumped out of bed so quickly, remembering I have a new feathered friend to feed.

As I walked on to the porch, he looked at me and made a loud falcon call, as if to say, *"Where have you been?" I am waiting for breakfast!"*!

From then on, everyday, I went out to feed him and talk with him. He even allowed the younger children, Oliva, and Ian, to pet him and hold him.

Although, Illya Marie, enjoyed watching at a distance. Oliva sat in the chair on the porch with the falcon perched beside her.

As she sat there talking with him, he seemed to listen intensely to what Oliva was saying. The falcon seemed to enjoy her words while she was petting him so softly.

Oliva made a connection with the falcon. It was as if they were long time best friends.

Ian did not hesitate to take his turn to sit and talk with the falcon. He too enjoyed petting him.

Usually, Ian is afraid to be around strange creatures, but he was not afraid to put on a heavy glove and allow the beautiful falcon to perch on his hand.

He used the other hand, which had no glove to feel the sharpness of the falcon's talons.

Chapter 5

The Journey Ends

Many days had past, and I could see that he was getting stronger and more restless. I told him whenever he is ready to go, let me know.

After about a week he was making a fuss outside. I could hear him flapping his wings and squawking.

As we went out on the porch, he was flying around. We could see the excitement on the Falcon's face.

His wing was better and he could fly again. We all clapped and cheered for him. I then realized this was the end of our journey together.

The feeling of excitement was now overcome with sadness. It was clear what needed to be done. I asked him if he was ready to go.

It was as if he answered *"yes"* with his bird voice.

I lowered my hand so he could perch on my hand for the last time. As he perched on my hand, he sat there in a very proud and confident way.

It was hard not to be sad, but I was also very happy for him.

We began walking around the house to the back yard. I could not help but to look at him as we walked together.

I then said to him, "My friend, you can go anytime". He then looked at me with his big beautiful falcon eyes, and began making his bird call, as if to say goodbye.

He spread his large wings out and off he flew, all the while squawking with his bird call.

Was that his way of saying, *"Thank you!", or "I will miss you!"* maybe he was saying, *"Don't* worry, I will be OK now."

Chapter 6

Teacher of Trust

I never saw him again after he flew from my hand. From time to time I would hear the certain familiar bird call that I came to recognize. I believe it is him just flying by to say hello.

I must say I miss my amazing friend. I hope that he is doing well. It was a wonderful experience that will never be forgotten.

Maybe if we see him again, he will tell us about all his adventures he has had.

The children and I learned many things while our falcon friend was with us. *First,* we must be willing to help all those in need.

Second, all living things are willing to trust us, if we just give them a chance. *Finally,* even if we do not speak the same language, every living creature understands the language of love and kindness.

Fly Free Soaring Spirit.

End..

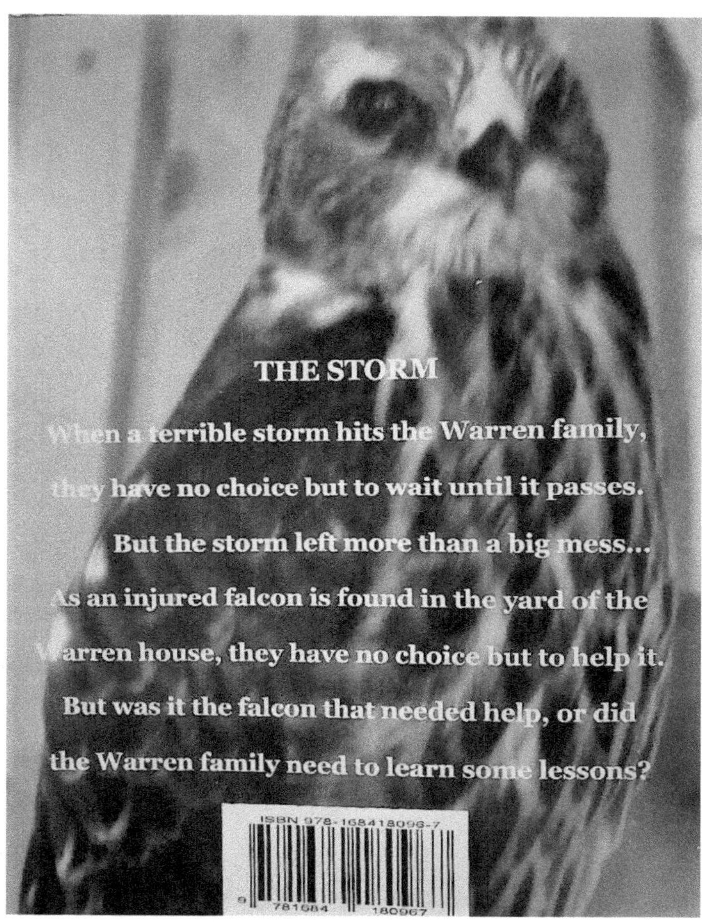
THE STORM

When a terrible storm hits the Warren family,

they have no choice but to wait until it passes.

But the storm left more than a big mess...

As an injured falcon is found in the yard of the

Warren house, they have no choice but to help it.

But was it the falcon that needed help, or did

the Warren family need to learn some lessons?

ISBN 978-1684180967

www.ingramcontent.com/pod-product-compliance
Lightning Source LLC
Chambersburg PA
CBHW051943150726
47999CB00006B/2340